Little Red Ric

A Fairy To

retold by Laura Layton Strom
illustrated by Bill Greenhead

Once upon a time, there was a little girl who lived in a village near some woods. Her grandmother had given her a red cloak as a gift, and she wore it everywhere. Soon people called her "Little Red Riding Hood" or even "Red."

2

Little Red Riding Hood wanted to visit her
grandmother. Grandmother lived deep in the
woods. Little Red Riding Hood gathered some
sweet-smelling, warm muffins in her basket. She
asked permission to go by herself this time.

"I'm very grown up now, you know," said Red. Her mother considered this. Little Red Riding Hood was getting older now, and she was a very bright girl.

"All right," said her mother. "But remember to go straight to Grandmother's house. Be alert, and don't talk to any strangers!" she warned.

"Don't worry, Mother," said Red.
"I'll be very careful."

Little Red Riding Hood set off into the forest with her basket of muffins. Before long she came to a clearing of beautiful wildflowers.

"Grandmother will like some fresh-picked flowers," she said to herself.

Forgetting her promise to her mother, she stopped and collected a bunch. She did not see the large shadow getting closer and closer.

A wolf appeared right beside her. At first Little Red Riding Hood was startled. But she loved all of the animals she had ever met. Then the wolf spoke in the friendliest voice he could do.

"Hello, my dear. What are you doing out here in the middle of the forest all by yourself?" Wolf asked.

"Oh, I'm on my way to visit my grandmother," said Red. "She lives about a mile up that way. In fact," she added, standing up, "I'm quite late so please excuse me." And Red rushed off toward Grandmother's house.

But Wolf knew a shortcut through the woods. He ran ahead and got to Grandmother's house before Little Red Riding Hood. Wolf hopped up onto Grandmother's porch and knocked on her door.

"Who is it?" called Grandmother.

"Little Red Riding Hood," said tricky Wolf in his best girl voice.

10

Grandmother opened the door and in came Wolf. He made one leap toward her, but she got away and hid in the closet.

Grandmother's bed cap lay on the floor, so Wolf picked it up and put it on. Then he slithered into the bedcovers and put Grandmother's glasses in front of his yellow eyes.

Soon Little Red Riding Hood arrived. "Hello, Grandmother!" she called.

"I'm in here," said Wolf in his best old woman voice.

"What big ears you have, Grandmother," said Red.

"The better to hear you with, my dear," said Wolf.

"What big eyes you have, Grandmother," said Red.

"The better to see you with, my dear," said Wolf.

"And what big teeth you have!" said Red.

"All the better to eat you with, my dear!"
And with that, Wolf jumped at Little Red Riding
Hood as she ran screaming, "Wolf! Wolf!"

A huntsman heard Little Red Riding Hood's
screams and came charging into the cottage.

The huntsman knocked Wolf unconscious and helped Grandmother out of the closet. She and Little Red Riding Hood were safe. The huntsman carried Wolf far away, where he wouldn't bother anyone again.

Little Red Riding Hood learned a valuable lesson.

Never, ever, ever talk to strangers!
And from that day forward, she never did.
And they all lived happily ever after.